The Underground GOATs

By

Brenda Wall

Cover design by JeDesignsGraphx™

Copyright c 2019 by Brenda Wall

First edition, first printing

Clay Court Publishing
Arlington

Printed in the United States of America

The Underground GOATs

By

Brenda Wall

The Underground GOATs

What a boring summer. It could have been great. It was supposed to be Hawaii or Disney World or at least basketball camp. But no. The family was headed to Portsmouth. Not the one in England either, but the one in Virginia. The one in Virginia was actually named for the one in England. I did not want to visit either one of them. I had no choice. It was not a vacation, even though my mother said it would be a good opportunity for us to have a family adventure. How could anyone have an adventure in Portsmouth?

She was good at putting a positive spin on things, but even she could not make this seem great to me.

So with little warning, we were packed and on the road. Our summer plans were suddenly cancelled so we could head south from our home in Washington, D.C. It was definitely disappointing, and I let everybody know how I felt. My dad said I needed to check my attitude. I heard him, but I just put on my headphones and got quiet.

I had pleaded to stay at home with my cousins, but my Mom said it would be too much of an imposition. I argued that I would be no trouble and it would be cheaper. I even said I was scheduled for the Sunday youth rotation at church, but she said Charles could stand in for me. There was no way out of this trip. So here we were in the van with my mother, father and younger brother on the four hour drive to Virginia.

The trip really wasn't all bad. We did get to stop on our road trip and have some of the best burgers ever near Richmond, Virginia. We soon saw the signs for Busch Gardens, and I said we should spend the night there, but we did not even stop for a snack. That might have been fun.

Like I said, the road trip part wasn't all bad, but I did not want to seem too happy. We always had good music in the car and Mom made sure the snacks were our favorites. We got to stop twice for breaks with more food and snacks. This was the best part of the *"adventure"* and we were getting closer and closer to the end. You could tell by the slow traffic. Once we passed Hampton University, I knew that we did not have far to go. Well, at least Harry and I could go swimming in the hotel pool when we got there.

Harry is my brother. He is three and he loves me. That is usually good. Sometimes, he tries to take my soccer ball or basketball and sometimes, he will want me to play my trumpet for him. My friends like him though and he is fine as long as I play with him, but he can also be very irritating. My mother is very patient with him, as you can imagine, because he is the baby. I wish she could be that patient with me, but she makes up for it when she lets me go with her on some of her trips. She goes to great places like St. Thomas in the Virgin Islands to visit her sister or to Florida. I guess my family likes the ocean, because we always seem to visit ocean destinations. I learned to swim by the time I was three because we spent so much time near water.

My dad also likes to go places, but when he takes me, we go because of his work. We live in Washington, D.C., near Howard University, which is where he was born. He was actually born in the same building where he later took classes. His father also lives in Washington and works at the African American Museum. It's called the National Museum of African American History and Culture. The first time I went there, I went with Ama. She is my grandmother and likes to go places, too. She lives in Atlanta and teaches at Morehouse College. Her son is my father. She is crazy about him and all of us, too. If I ask her at the right time, she will usually agree to buy me the latest sneakers, my favorite.

Back to the trip. I was still sulking. My father always says I need to adjust my attitude. But everyone knew I did not want to spend my vacation in this town when all of my friends were either home, at camp or on some wonderful trip. Why couldn't we go to Hawaii or New York City again or maybe the Grand Canyon? Portsmouth???!!! There would be nothing to do. Stuck in Portsmouth, Virginia with my father, baby brother and my mother.

The reason we had to make this trip is because of my grandmother, Ama. But even Ama was not going to be with us. What does that tell you? Ama grew up and even married my grandfather in Portsmouth, which is an old, historic city. Because she grew up there, she knew about some of its history. Portsmouth was scouted around the time that captured Africans were first brought to this land against their will. Slavery. She talked a lot about slavery and freedom. Portsmouth was originally settled as a plantation colony, because it was near the water. That means they needed the free labor that came from enslavement. It doesn't look like much of a river today, but the waterway was very important a few hundred years ago.

Today, you can catch the ferry between Portsmouth and Norfolk, which I have done before; it takes about fifteen minutes. Anyway, the city was founded because of the waterways that the Powhatan Indians used for travel and trade back then. Remember the movie, Pocahontas? Chief Powhatan was the name of her father. Their home was not far away in what was re-named Jamestown.

Portsmouth did eventually develop a naval shipyard, with lots of ships either being built or repaired, but it was not even named the Portsmouth Shipyard. It was named for Norfolk. That's the historic part. There's more involving the Civil War and the decision to burn the shipyard so that it would not fall into Confederate hands, even though the capital of the confederacy was in Virginia, but I fear I have lost you already. I know a lot of facts from reading and from YouTube, not to mention Ama. I'm getting to be as boring as Portsmouth.

Well, we were getting closer. We were passing Norfolk State University, which is just across the Elizabeth River on our way to Portsmouth. My great grandfather was a chemistry professor there. They said everyone loved him.

Almost there. The reason we are all going on this trip is because Miss Churchill, a teacher who knew the family, left a will that was recently discovered. The will was written a long time ago, when Ama was in college, but they had just found it. It was in some boxes of books that Miss Churchill donated to the church that never got unpacked. I don't know how that happened, but we *are in the will.* By that I mean, my grandmother is in it and we are her heirs. Ama said that we could have whatever. Maybe we will be rich! That could be exciting.

Maybe, we could move into a mansion and I could pay someone to do my chores. Boy, I would never have to do chores again. We could have a swimming pool in the back yard or maybe even in the house. I would go to all the basketball games and maybe even take trips with the team. This could be great. This trip might be the greatest thing to happen to me.

Back to reality. Ama was somewhere in Ghana on a study trip with her students. She was old, but no one seemed to notice. Everybody did call her *mother* as a way of showing respect. She loved it when they did this, but said she had to be careful about age discrimination. It was not a missionary trip, but more of a cultural exchange with a social justice twist. *Missionaries are what kept Africa colonized.* That usually got a reaction from her church friends. If they were too shaken, she might add,

"But what they meant for evil, God meant for good." It was a quote from Genesis.

Ama is really into liberation and justice, probably because she grew up in the South when things were pretty bad. She went to segregated schools, segregated hospitals and they even had colored and white water fountains. She said they called African Americans *"colored,"* when she was born. Negro was another name they used to be more proper.

Miss Churchill was a history teacher, who taught all of Ama's family but not Ama. For some reason, Miss Churchill loved my grandmother, when she was in school. I think they were both born in October. Miss Churchill taught her whole life and never had any children. Teachers were not allowed to be married back then. Before she stopped teaching, she moved into a new house across the street from Ama. That's how they became friends. Miss Churchill was a descendant of Thomas Jefferson and Sally Hemings, but that was before they had DNA evidence. She just knew about it from her parents and great grandparents.

That was long after the Africans came to Virginia and the Powhatan lost much of their land. Thomas Jefferson had children with Sally Hemings, who was also enslaved. She was very pretty, but was just a teenager when Jefferson was old. They had a lot of slavery in Virginia. It was really bad back then.

Today we were headed to the hotel so we could unpack and get something to eat. It was nothing like the big hotels at home, but it was nice. They actually had a picture of Miss Churchill in the hotel lobby. They had some other old pictures, too. I wondered if Ama's friends were in any of them. The hotel was on the waterfront, so we had a good view of the river and could see Norfolk on the other side. They had television for my parents and Wi-Fi for us; I had my phone and iPad, so I could watch my basketball highlights. Malcolm was my favorite player and of course, I loved LeBron. Even Ama loved him, especially after he opened his school. She doesn't know much about sports and I am pretty sure that the only time she has gone to a basketball game was when she took me once or when I was playing in my youth league.

My parents would go to the church and meet with the lawyers. I was ready to go to the pool before dinner, but my Dad said we did not have time to go swimming now. What?!! He said something about my attitude again, which was typical, but now he was turning into our tour guide. He was going on about how 1619 was not really the first time enslaved Africans came to the Americas, but it was recognized as the beginning of slavery in Virginia. My family was really into our history and I knew better than to be sarcastic.

Before I could change into my new jeans and my favorite sneakers, our parents said we had to go with them to the church. *Not church while we are on vacation*! I liked church okay, but this was not my church. Emanuel AME Church was the church where they found the will. Miss Churchill taught Sunday school there and also taught a lot of the church courses. She must have been a pretty special teacher to have her picture in the hotel lobby. It seems that they found the will in one of the old books she donated to the church a long time ago. It was lost in boxes stored at the church long after she died. Well, the lawyer was going to meet with the family and some of the others named in the will. They were supposed to be there at seven o'clock. That meant we had to get dragged there, too. We had to go because they did not want to leave us alone at the hotel. Boring just got worse, but at least I had my phone.

The church was not far from the hotel. When we got there, it looked pretty much like a modern church, but the stained glass windows did not seem very new. In fact, the closer you got, it almost did not seem to match. The inside looked older and not modern at all. The pews were wooden and when you went into the sanctuary, the pulpit had a lot of wood and there were pipes from a pipe organ. Everybody was very friendly and it seemed like a regular church. However, this church was really old.

You could tell the building was old if you looked more closely at the stained glass. The balcony, floors and pews were built by both enslaved and free African Americans before the Civil War. That was the war that ended enslavement. The iron works were original, too. My father told me that this church was used in the Underground Railroad.

The Underground Railroad was not a train, but secret hiding places all the way from the South, where enslavement was allowed, to freedom in the north, where there was no enslavement. Because Emanuel was so close to the harbor, those brave enough to risk escaping enslavement had people who were willing to help them. The people who came through here could hide under the pulpit or in the attic of the church.

They would then flee to box cars and finally hide on ships in the Elizabeth River. The ships would then head north, until they reached states, where there was no slavery. They would be free (if they weren't caught again and brought back South).

This church was founded in 1792 by the African Methodist Society and their white counterparts. They met separately until Nat Turner's Rebellion in 1831, which was not too far away from Portsmouth. His fight for freedom scared everybody, which meant that the African Methodist Society was forced to meet with the white Methodists. A lot of important history, which really was not so boring. Thoughts of freedom were always at hand, which explains the dangerous risk of Emanuel Church in helping enslaved families escape to freedom. That had to be hard because they still required white supervision even though they had their own church. Slavery was horrible.

That was interesting, but I still had my basketball highlights to watch. So when my parents went in with the lawyers and pastor, I waited for them in the church sanctuary. My phone battery was getting low, so I looked for an outlet to recharge my phone. That's when my boring story became unbelievable.

Chapter Two

I found an outlet for my phone near the pulpit.
If I stretched up, I could reach it from the floor.
But when I reached for my phone, I accidentally
pushed it into a hole near the lectern, which had
an oversized Bible on it. I had to get my phone,
but I could not reach it or pull it back out by the
cord. When I found one of the members and
asked where my phone had fallen, she said
probably into the furnace room, which was
under the pulpit. I would have to go find it. I was
not really upset, but I made Harry go with me so
that we could stay together. He had his ball so

he did not mind going with me. I found the room under the pulpit and saw my phone. Luckily, it did not break because it was still attached to the cord. Thank goodness.

I got the phone and was ready to go when Harry started to panic. His ball had rolled behind some old boxes. (I wonder if this was more of Miss Churchill's generosity.) We both could see the ball, but could not get to it. The boxes were too heavy to move, so I let Harry crawl and try to get it. He might be able to squeeze in because he was smaller. When he grasped the ball, he tripped forward and fell. I could not see him. I tried to get to him, and that's when I also fell into a dark, wet hole. I was in trouble now, but I could feel Harry and tried to reach his arm.

Harry didn't cry, because of the shock. I tried to keep myself from crying when I realized our danger. We could not climb up, because there was no way to reach the edge. And I was not strong enough to lift Harry over my head. No one could hear us when we yelled for help. We could not be that far away from the church sanctuary, but still no one answered. I turned on my phone light and made sure that Harry was okay. Since no one could hear us, I thought I had better find a way out before my parents realized we were not where we were supposed to be. It had only been a few minutes, so I knew we had enough time.

When Harry asked me for some gum, I gave him my last piece. I hoped that would distract him, while I was thinking. Then I saw a light in the distance. It was probably another room and I thought that we could find our way back to the sanctuary from there. We were not hurt so we crawled towards the light, through a cramped enclosure, which got brighter. I started to feel relieved, when I discovered an old door which I pushed open.

I guess they were having a church program, because the two men in the room had on costumes. They were not very tall and looked like they were dressed the way they did in history books. I could hear them whispering and when they saw us they were startled and became quiet.

"What are you doing here? Who is with you?"

I started to tell them that my parents were in the meeting with the pastor, when the shorter man with the beard left and looked to see where we had been. When he did not see anyone, he seemed to be rather frantic in the way he searched behind us. The other man, started to look around at the other side of the room, and threw the chairs back to see if anyone else was around.

They both got quiet, but then the first man started to grab my arm and roughly pull me away from Harry. Harry knew there was danger and he suddenly screamed and threw his ball at the man across the room. The ball missed the man but hit a picture on the wall, which came crashing down. The noise distracted both men and the man who was holding my arm dropped his hold. Harry and I immediately started to pull away and run away from them. This was all happening so fast. I could not figure out who these people were, but it was clear that they were dangerous. Maybe they were kidnappers. But kidnappers at church? In costumes? Harry and I ran towards what I thought was the parking lot, when two other men came from behind some wooden stairs and grabbed us.

One whispered for us to be quiet and follow them. The other man took Harry's hand and said we were going to be safe. We did what they said and I was hoping we would soon be outside. However, they slipped us up the stairs to a small, hiding place. We were all quiet, but could hear the two men yelling that they had lost us. They ran outside thinking that's where we ran. We could hear them still chasing us at first and then by the time we were well hidden upstairs, we could no longer hear them. At least we were still in the church. With so much noise and confusion, I could not understand why our parents did not come and check on us. They always made sure we were doing what we were supposed to be doing.

After a few more moments of silence, the two men who helped us started to laugh.

"We got away again. This is getting a little too close."

They then started to talk to us and ask us exactly the same questions we heard before.

"What are you doing here? Who is with you?"

The other man seemed friendlier and asked

"What's your name and how did you find us?"

I tried to tell him that my name was David, but he was not listening. He kept searching the room and watching all around us. Harry was quiet and sitting very close to me. We knew we were in trouble, but we felt safe with these two men. I told him that I was trying to get my phone, when Harry fell behind the furnace.

He seemed confused and could not understand what I was saying.

"What do you mean, 'phone?'"

When I asked him if he could take us back to the sanctuary, he told us that was not safe for us. That did not make sense to me, but maybe that's where the other men were checking. Anyway, I tried to quietly call my father on the cell phone, but the call did not go through. I felt like crying, but I did not want Harry to worry. I tried again, but no phone reception. This was really bad.

The other man who helped us could tell we were both upset. He said everything was going to be fine. He smiled and said,

"Trouble don't last always."

He seemed very calm and confident. He said the men who were chasing us were from the white Methodist church. They were making sure that *the slaves* were not causing *freedom trouble* at Emanuel. I was still having problems understanding the play, the church and why those men were so mean to Harry and me.

The kind man said his name was Nathan. He was Nathan Jones and the man with him was his brother, Arthur Jones. They were from North Carolina and were visiting members of Emanuel. I heard them say that they had cut the trees for the benches. Now that seemed strange since the original benches were over two hundred years old. Still strange. I heard them say they had to move the benches for church, because they were not allowed to sit in the *white* pews even when they were required to go to the white Methodist church. So they took their benches with them. I was beginning to feel curious about Mr. Nathan and Mr. Arthur, but I was even more worried about being away from my parents.

It was still light outside, when we heard the church bell ring. And by that I mean bells. The church bells started to ring and it was very loud because we were actually under the church belfry. That's where they keep the bell.

When that happened, Nathan and Arthur got excited. (They must really be religious.) They told us we had to go with them now and they both started to move fast. Nathan grabbed my hand and the other man asked Harry if he could carry him. Before we could answer, we were leaving our hiding place. I felt like they were honest and trying to keep us safe, but what about our parents? With no questions asked, they took us outside. I was glad because the car would be there on the parking lot, but I was also afraid the mean men might try to get us.

The men who were helping us started to hum to us. I had heard the tune before. I could tell they were being serious and still trying to keep us calm. *"Swing low, sweet chariot."* That was the tune that Ama sang to us, but I did not feel like singing or humming.

When we got outside, there were no cars, no parking lot, but instead lots of trees. Two women and three children met us and did not seem at all surprised that we were with the men. As it turned out, they had been hiding in the church behind the choir loft. Everyone was wearing the costumes from the play.

When we got outside, everything was different. It smelled different. You could smell salt in the air and it was quiet. The families were calm, as they hurried and gathered us with their own children. We were walking fast, running and hiding. We were soon getting onto boxcars, which looked like a cross between trains and busses, but there were no cars, no traffic and no streets with curbs or sidewalks. Instead there were a few horses and some of the horse drawn carriages like the ones you see for tourists. Harry was now holding my hand, but no longer seemed scared. I looked for more gum but had none to give him.

The two ladies could tell we were confused and worried and they started talking softly to us.

"We did not realize that there were other children who would be going with us. Where are you from?"

We told them that we were from Washington, D.C. and then they seemed puzzled.

"Do you mean that you are going to Washington?"

They turned to Nathan and said,

"But Washington is the other way. Why are they here?"

Before we could explain, we were all riding. It was a bumpy ride. I was getting scared again. There was no hotel, there were no cars and my phone was not working. Harry was so close that he was sitting on me and I was glad. What was happening?

There was not time to explain. We were told to be quiet and the other children had not said anything for all this time so we got quiet, too. The two boys seemed around my age and the girl was about five. We soon reached our stop and we got off to head toward a docked boat. Not the ferry, but a small ship. They signaled Nathan to come on board, but I could tell we were still being careful. We made it. Once we were hidden away, the questions and answers started.

They wanted to know why we were dressed the way we were. They were very curious about our shoes. Nikes. Both of us. Nathan figured we were free because of the way I talked and I had read a store sign. He told me to be quiet when he heard me read the signs. It was attracting attention. They were not allowed to learn to read when they were enslaved. He was also very curious about my watch and the light I had used on my phone. There was no light in our small room and I used the light to help Harry tie his shoes. Nathan was fascinated by this.

When we were alone, the ladies told us we had to change clothes because we needed to blend in when we reached our destination. I heard them say we were headed to Boston. I got excited because I had been to nearby Martha's Vineyard and maybe could find my godparents. They were not interested and had never heard of Martha's Vineyard.

I was getting hungry. When I asked for a hamburger, I realized that was a stupid request. The ladies offered us some bread and some fig preserves. I wasn't *that* hungry. Harry was. He ate a sandwich that was fashioned out of the bread pieces and preserves. He liked it.

I was becoming less worried because these families were so kind. But was this a dream? It was taking me a while to consider that I had fallen back into a time warp. I was back during slavery time. And somehow, being free seemed as unsafe as being enslaved. I guess I was free. I was learning more, but it was getting dark. Since it was summer, I figured that it was getting late. My watch still worked and it said it was nine o'clock. Harry was falling asleep on me, but I was still hyped.

I did have to go to the bathroom, which was a problem. They told me I had to go to the part of the ship that opened outside. That was okay for now, but I hated to think about what would happen when more was involved. I was learning about slop jars, which I had never heard of before. Where was air freshener when you needed it?

The gentle roll of the ocean was having its effect on me. I was soon falling asleep on Harry. The next day would bring another even more bewildering development.

Chapter Three

The next morning started when it was still dark. Harry was crying softly and I told him we were fine. We forgot to sing the Lord's Prayer last night so I was quietly singing it to him. The other two boys heard me and came over near us. We had not spoken at all until now. When we got to the end, *the power and the glory forever. Amen,* they started singing with us. It made me feel good. As it turned out, they were listening to us all along. They were not the children of Mr. Nathan and Mr. Arthur; they were being sheltered by them just like we were. They were not enslaved, free or from Portsmouth. They were from Atlanta, which was deep in the South, but they knew about Morehouse. They read it on Harry's shirt before he covered it with the cotton tunic they gave us. That meant that they could also read. Interesting. That was even more curious because Morehouse had not yet been founded. We were now living well before the Civil War, which did not end until—I forgot. But I did know the Emancipation Proclamation was in 1863.   We were back in the time of legal slavery. How could they know about Morehouse? Maybe the same way I did.

I did not say anything, but now was my turn to listen. Both of the boys could read. They were both twelve. One was Bill and the other was David, which was my name, too. They looked like they could be my cousins. In fact, David looked just like my cousin Randall. What a coincidence! As it turned out, there was a coincidence, but that was not it. Bill and David were both from Atlanta and came to Portsmouth on a trip with their school. They were visiting college summer programs and had gone to Hampton University and Norfolk State University. They came to Emanuel because someone told them about the historic Underground Railroad.

When they were looking for a water fountain, they noticed an opening in the choir loft and investigated. The next thing they knew, they were separated from their group and alone. It was not until the preacher found them that they realized that they were not only separated from their group, but they were also in a different time and space. For some reason, they were calm and not at all frightened. They had been watching us and seemed to be very patient with us. When Harry got more annoying, they laughed and played with him. They were as patient with him as my mother. I saw that Harry was even chewing gum, which he no doubt got from one of them. I had to remind him not to take gifts from strangers, but everybody was a stranger now.

And then I heard the most amazing conversation. They loved Calvin Hill and the Dallas Cowboys. Now, I remember Calvin Hill from my football magazines. He was Grant Hill's father. He was also a freshman at Yale when my grandfather graduated. That was a long time ago, everybody, but not that long. Not before the Civil War! Hmmmm. Strange but not so scary. Bill seemed to know more. He seemed to be the fact person; he was very serious and did not smile much, but he knew everything. David seemed to be the kind one, who had a great sense of humor. He could even make Bill laugh. He was funny, kind and smart. He is the one who gave Harry the gum. For some reason, both Harry and I were drawn to them. When the adults were around, both of them were as quiet as I was. Harry was the only one who was laughing, playing with a new toy made of rags and asking for more goodies. It was working. He was now eating a juicy apple.

I needed to know more about where I was, who these other two boys were and how I was going to get back to my parents. Not to mention that we were at risk of being enslaved! I never really thought about what that would be like or that my family had to deal with slavery, segregation and racism.

Bill said that he was an Eagle Scout and that his father had taught him a lot about his family. His father sounded as cool as my father. His father had been to a lot of colleges and was personally chastised by George Washington Carver for being too loud in the dorm when he was a student at Tuskegee University. It would be a while before he settled down, but when he did, he knew just about every African American intellectual in the Harlem Renaissance from Sterling Brown to Charles Houston and also some of the famous ones you would know. Anyway, Bill thought his father was great, but all this was well after slavery. Bill was the one who was talking about Calvin Hill.

David said he had a brilliant father, but he grew up with his mother, who was just wonderful. Both of his parents went to prestigious schools and spent their lives focused on family and community. They believed in liberation, loved learning and loved life. David's mother lived in the world differently; his father was more traditional in his life choices. This combined to produce great DNA. They were all deep thinkers and very compassionate. David did not talk very much about history, but instead told family stories.

It was a minute before I realized that these stories were very familiar ones. They were my stories. Could Bill and David be my relatives? My father and grandfather? David seemed to know who Bill was, but Bill had no idea who David was. Neither knew who Harry or I were, but they sure did like us. You could tell. You know, I think I was looking at my father and grandfather when they were around my age. Now *that* was crazy! Wow!

Chapter Four

I was getting sea sick by the time everyone got us ready in the middle of the night. It was really dawn. They told us we would soon be leaving the ship and I helped get our things together. I don't think any of us knew where we were, but everybody onboard sure was happy. We were above the Mason-Dixon Line, whatever that was. What they told us was that we were now free. Free at last! I was glad to be in Boston, but I soon found out that we were nowhere near Boston. We were in Pennsylvania and would be leaving the ship in Philadelphia. That was good news too, because my godmother lived there. We had family everywhere. We did not have to hide when we left the ship in the same way, but we still had to make sure that we did not attract too much attention.

Soon we were leaving the boat and headed to another church to get some food and find others who would help us. It was another AME church in downtown Philadelphia. It was the next safe place. From here, we would meet others and leave church with new families. The name on the sign said *Mother Bethel AME Church.* Wait! I was there last Christmas with my godmother!!!! Now it did not look the same, but I remembered the name of the street. In fact, I was in Erin's wedding there, when I was two. I took a tour of the church after one of the Sunday services and remembered that they had a museum in the basement.

This was another historic church, founded in 1787. That was after the American Revolution in 1776 and long before the Civil War. I wondered if they used the same furniture that I saw in the basement museum. I just wasn't paying that much attention on the tour. This time the whole church seemed to be in the basement. The building was much smaller and not much larger than the ground floor.

I heard David tell Bill that he had visited Mother Bethel, too. He said his godparents lived in Philadelphia and took him to church on Christmas Eve. He was excited, but Bill was not very impressed.

When we got inside the church, we were able to wash ourselves, get something to eat and find out what was next. The grown-ups were reading some kind of reports and exchanging letters. The little girl was sitting near them.

There would be new families who would take care of us, but we would now have to split up. Mr. Nathan and Mr. Arthur would make sure we were safe and then they would head back to North Carolina in a couple of days. They said Harry and I would stay together and the ladies and their daughter would stay together with a different family. Harry had played with the little girl when we were on the boat and she was very sweet to him, but very proper. He would probably miss her. I didn't even know her name, but they called her "Little Miss O." She waved at me and gave Harry a hug goodbye. She said something to him when she left, but I did not hear her and really did not pay much attention. I was too worried.

I did not know what to do. Should I try to go with Mr. Nathan and Mr. Arthur and get closer to Portsmouth or should I stay with the family who would take care of us in Philadelphia? I was safe now, but I was still away from my real family. I was not only missing them, but I was getting very scared. I was really praying and keeping Harry close to me. He was fine, because he did not understand what was happening. That's when David and Bill started to talk to me.

Chapter Five

Bill suggested that the four of us should try to stay together. That's when he told us how he ended up with us. He was not really from Atlanta, but was visiting family there. He was from Washington, D.C., too. He was at Emanuel, because his family was using it as a rest stop, when they were on a family trip from Washington to Atlanta. Remember, travel through the South was dangerous during segregation and this church was a safe place to stop, use the restrooms and get directions. He was alone, when he was looking for a printing press that he heard was in the church basement. Bill and his father actually had a printing press in their basement at home and used it to print flyers, announcements and invitations. Bill wanted to see what kind of type they had. The church sexton was showing Bill, when he left thinking he heard someone calling for him. What he found was his first trip Underground. He had been to Portsmouth when he was a child and he had returned twice to help. He had been Underground before!

That's when Bill told me not to worry. He said that I would be with my family before I knew it. I was not sure what he meant when he said he came to help, but it seemed that every time he came back to Portsmouth, he was able to bring information, which would help those escaping to freedom. When he returned to his own real time, he would read everything on freedom and the Civil War and then use that information to help families when he came back through the portal in Portsmouth. When he came back, he was always twelve on the Underground, but he had been back twice.

In his time Bill was now twenty one. He had just graduated from Yale with a double major in mathematics and a new experimental major in African American Studies. No wonder he knew everything. This was his last visit. He told me that he was here to make sure enslavement would end, which he knew it would, and to save as many lives as he could. And then he said something very interesting:

He was on a mission to make sure that the country would survive in the future with freedom for all!

He was living during a time when there was a lot of racial turmoil and freedom fighting in this country and also throughout Africa. By helping freedom fighters and their families during this era, he said it would make a difference in the future. So that explains why he knew Calvin Hill. However, what he did not know was anything that happened after 1970. That's why he did not recognize Harry or me, because we were not born in 1970. He did not know about David, either. However, he did know Ama. No wonder they were always talking about freedom. No wonder she sang *Swing Low Sweet Chariot.* No wonder they loved the church and taught us about prayer.

I started to laugh when I realized that Bill was my grandfather. He did not know it, but I started teasing him. Bill, that was funny just calling him that.

"Is your girlfriend smart?"

He was twelve, but he knew everything up to

when he was grown at twenty one. He ignored me.

"Is your girlfriend pretty?"

 I was asking questions about Ama and no one knew this was funny but me. I thought it was hilarious.

"Is your girlfriend a good cook?"

I knew the answer to that one and laughed out loud. I knew about him, but he did not know about me. What about David?

David was eating some fruit and some chicken over by the window, which was the very best food the church members had. They also had some cake that was delicious! I asked David how he knew Bill. He knew that Bill was his father, but he realized that Bill did not know him. He was not yet born when Bill was twenty one. Bill was just graduating from college and was about to get married to David's mother, my Ama. But David did not know about Harry or me either, because we were not born when he came through the portal in Portsmouth.

David explained that he first met Bill on this trip through the portal, which was his second trip. He came back this time because he wanted to make sure that his family would be safe in the future. When he came the first time, he did not leave Portsmouth, but discovered that some of the people on the Underground could not swim and were in danger of drowning when the boats encountered turbulent weather. It was his task to make sure those on the Underground learned how to use CPR. They needed to know how to revive, or resuscitate, those who stopped breathing, when they panicked and drowned. That would depend on Ama's grandfather, who was Nathan Jones.

So Nathan Jones was Ama's grandfather! He was a strong swimmer and spent a lot of time swimming and fishing. I even saw the tool he used to repair fishing nets. Ama had it. David had to show Nathan how to do CPR and make it seem natural. That would be difficult. CPR would be necessary for the Underground, but also for Ama's family. It would determine whether our family would survive.

David had gotten to know Nathan on the last trip, when he was cutting trees for the benches. When he got hot and wanted to take a break, they went swimming in a nearby creek. They pulled off their shoes, rolled up their pant legs and took off their shirts. It was so cool and nice. About an hour later, some white bullies came and said racist, cruel things to them. They were getting ready to leave when one of the white boys came after them in the creek. The bully slipped and went under. Can you believe it? He couldn't swim. Nathan got to him and pulled him from the water. But he wasn't breathing! That was David's chance. The other friend was scared and crying, but David turned him over onto his back and started to do CPR. Nathan was watching and was worried that David might be hurting his ribs. David didn't stop and said it was fine. After about a minute, the waterlogged boy, started to cough. He did not know what had happened and he was disoriented. His friend was confused, but was trying his best to say thank you. That was hard for him, because the ones who saved his friend were Black.

Nathan left with David and you can be sure that Nathan had a lot of questions about what happened. In the next couple of days he told many of his friends what happened and several of them practiced CPR on each other. They would save many lives, including one child, who was thrown from an overturned boat; this child would grow up to become Ama's grandmother. David's mission was accomplished.

I agreed to stay with Bill and David and not try to leave with Mr. Nathan and Mr. Arthur. I did not realize it, but this would be when we would say our last goodbye to them. I started to cry when Mr. Nathan hugged Harry and me. He smiled and said to me,

"Remember little son, trouble don't last always!"

He then took out a fancy, ornamental cross and gave it to Harry. He told Harry to let me carry it for him because it was so heavy. He said that he made it from some of the left over iron from the church in Portsmouth. He engraved his favorite saying on it: *Trouble don't last always.* He made me promise to keep it with me.

"It will keep you safe and when you need it most, it will remind you of your faith. You and Harry will be just fine."

I did cry a little more. I was still not sure I was making the right decision even though Bill said I would be able to get home soon.

Chapter Six

The four of us left the church and went to a small house not far from downtown. The couple who took us in were older and had grown children. They also had a dog named Rex. They loved Harry and he did make us laugh a lot. Harry loved Rex and made a toy for him out of his own toy made from rags. They told us that we would all sleep in one room. They showed us how we could wash up and of course, they told us about the slop pot. They called it a chamber pot. We would use it to dispose of the water we used to brush our teeth and wash with. We did not have tooth brushes, but we had soap; we would have to use cloth and salt for cleaning our teeth. We would use the chamber pot when we had to go to the bathroom at night. Yuck! And then one of our chores was to take it outside and clean it for the next night. They told us about our other chores and how we could help them when we were there. I liked them. Harry did too, but he had a problem when the lady spanked his hand for not listening. And then she spanked it again when he cried too loudly. This was new to him and he did not like it. But he did like her apple pie and he was soon better, when she gave him a big slice.

When we went to bed, we talked some more. We said our prayers first and Harry fell asleep next to me. I was glad that he was fine. He kept asking about our parents and I reminded him that we were on a vacation adventure. He liked the boat ride and he liked all the new people we were meeting. I let him hold the special cross when he fell asleep. Bill, David and I talked more about how to get home.

Fortunately, both of them had been home before so they were not worried at all. They were more focused on why they were back in time and how they were helping their family and their future. Bill wanted to protect the future for our people and David wanted to keep the family safe. Both were being very successful. David had introduced CPR to people who needed it most. And Bill was getting information to those who were escaping to freedom. I just wanted to go home.

That's when they said that everyone who came through the Underground portal had a special purpose. Bill was here to provide information. David was here to save lives. Why were Harry and I here?

Chapter Seven

Everyone was tired, but for some reason Harry was still up and talking to all of the adults. There was no enslavement in Philadelphia, but it could still be dangerous for those who were fighting for freedom. They were called abolitionists and it was not always very safe or popular. Some of the families who helped lost jobs and sometimes they could even be kidnapped and taken deep into the South and enslaved. The people who caught them were evil, and they also did it to make money.

They told me about one free man, who was enslaved for twelve years before he was able to be freed. He was captured on a trip to Washington, D.C. His family thought he was dead so you know they were glad to see him after twelve years. That was a long time to be enslaved, but think about those who would never be free. Slavery was horrible, but adults did not discuss it a lot around the children. They wanted the children to feel safe and grow up feeling protected, even when the children were escaping to freedom. Even with us the grown-ups would whisper about things that were "not for children's ears." In this way it was easier to keep the secrets safe and better control the danger.

We were told not to discuss our trip and not to tell anyone where we were from. We would be introduced as family coming to visit for the rest of the summer. They did not want the secret of the Underground Railroad to get into the wrong hands. They told us how important this was at the church and again with our new family. It was very important for children to obey adults. There was no back talk and children seemed to be much quieter around adults. It could be very dangerous if a child said the wrong thing.

I know my father said I needed to check my attitude, but now I knew how important it was to listen and cooperate. My job was to take care of Harry and make sure we got back home. I could not see any purpose beyond that.

Everyone loved Harry and they thought he was very smart. He seemed to bring laughter and joy when he was around. Even the serious preacher at church seemed more relaxed when he met Harry. When he introduced us to the congregation, he said we represented the future and they would not stop working until they knew that all of the children would be free. He again said we were the future. Then Harry stood up, took a bow and everyone laughed, including the stern ladies, who never seemed to smile.

I guess that was a gift that Harry had. He made people remember how to relax. The preacher called it peace. I called it love. I sure loved Harry and felt better when he was with me. Even when we argued at home, I still liked it when he was around. So if Harry's purpose was to help others calm down and feel normal, even when there was great danger, what was my mission?

I could read, but that did not seem to be it. Nobody needed me to read anything for them. I decided that maybe the best way I could help was to do chores and cooperate. So I made sure Harry was safe and then asked how I could help. It was not long before I was washing clothes, getting wood, painting the fence and cleaning chamber pots. Yuck!

Remember, there were no washing machines. Instead of a washer, there was a large metal tub for washing. The water had to be heated on the stove and then poured into the tub. And the stove was not like ours; it was a stove that used fire from wood to make the heat. That meant that I had to get the wood to put in the stove and also clean the ashes from the stove.

Soap and vinegar were used in the water to wash clothes. Also washboards were used to rub the clothes clean. I would then rinse in another tub, wring the clothes and hang them on the line to dry. This was a lot of heavy work and my hands got blisters, but I was determined to help. We would play in the water, too. The first time we washed clothes, Harry and I both got really wet and had to let the clothes we were wearing dry, too. It was fun and it kept me from thinking about home.

We did not have real lunch. Instead we ate some fruit, cheese and bread. I didn't like milk, so they let me drink cool water. Dinner was delicious. We had homemade biscuits, stew, collard greens and homemade applesauce. I guess the food was the best part. I really appreciated the home cooking and my new family appreciated all of my help. They said I was a natural leader.

"There is dignity in work," they said.

Bill and David were not around very much because they were a little older. They were allowed to leave with the grown-ups. I don't know where they went, but I got the impression that they went to work with the adults and also attend their community meetings. They met with other abolitionists and could learn from them. We all had a part to play and it was working.

Chapter Eight

We were doing fine. The chores were done, but Harry was getting more homesick from being away from our parents. So was I. We had a good time last night though. The family had a party for us. They had a piano, so we had music, singing, dancing and food. We started out singing church songs, before the tambourines really came out and they asked us what our favorite songs were. Harry started with "*Kiki, do you love me...*" He was doing his dance and everybody was laughing and trying to join in. Bill said his song was *Don't Mess with Bill*. Everybody thought he was making it up, but I knew better. We sure had fun.

We went to bed late, but I always said my prayers. I prayed for my whole family, plus my new family and freedom, too. I really missed my mom. I had the best mother in the world. When I was sick, she would sleep on the floor next to my bed so she could make sure I was comfortable. And she loved to have surprises for the family. I fell asleep thinking about how she always solved our family problems. How would she want me to solve this problem?

We were tired the next day. We had to get up early before church to help with breakfast. When we were getting ready, I put my tee shirt on under our new clothes and told Harry he could wear his Morehouse shirt under his new clothes, too. We also wore our sneakers, which was good since we had to walk quite a distance. Harry wanted to take our cross with us. Since we were going to church, I thought it would be fine, even though it was heavy. We had to walk to church and it was not too far, but it still took us about an hour to get there. It was our first Sunday since getting back and we had to go to church. That was not optional. I was tired, but wanted to go. Maybe God would help us get back home. I had to try.

The church was hot, but there was a cool breeze every now and then. The music was familiar and everyone sang, but the sermon was pretty long.

They welcomed us and made us feel good. The two ladies and O were at church, too. It was good to see them. Harry went over to sit with O after the service. It looked like she was reading something to Harry and I could see them talking to each other.

Bill, David and I were talking some more about the work they were doing to help. Bill wanted to make sure that he was sharing his information, but not everyone was ready to listen to a twelve year old. David had already been pretty successful on his mission so he was more relaxed. It was all important help for the Underground Railroad, but I had to confess that I really wanted to go home.

That's when they asked me how I was helping. I told them about my new chores and how I was learning to get wood, start the stove, heat water, wash clothes, keep the chamber pots clean, read some of the old books in the house and always take care of Harry.

That's when Bill said that there was something very special about being able to help others who were changing history. Because of the bravery of the people we were helping, people who were mean and sick with racism would soon have an opportunity to get better. But for sure, our family and community would be the leaders in changing the world. They said I had an opportunity to be a part of this change. *But how?*

And then they said the most amazing thing! They said they could tell I was very smart, very responsible and very kind. They watched the way I took care of Harry. That was natural for me, but they said that was a sign that I was a leader. That was my special gift. They also said that was how I would learn my way home. It would come when I was *naturally* leading.

Chapter Nine

Well, it was time to leave for home with my new family. Harry was still playing with O, but he was ready to go. I know he was tired for the long walk home, so I told him he could have a piggy back ride to start. We were still in the church when O told him to remember what she had said to him. He laughed, jumped onto my back and we started to look for our new family. When we got near the door, Harry dropped the cross. We were always losing things in the church. Harry got down so we could look for it, but it was nowhere around. Harry thought he found it, but what he found was his ball. Remember, the one he threw so we could get away in Portsmouth?

When I asked him to show me where he found the ball, he did. It was on the other side of the closet door. I thought the cross could be inside, too. We both looked in the darkened closet. It wasn't there, but when we came out, we were back at Emanuel Church in Portsmouth. How did that happen? Bill and David were gone, our new family was gone and so was Mother Bethel Church in Philadelphia.

Harry said we were back, because we were brave and good. I guess he had faith. He said O told him the ball was her present to him. She also told Harry that he and I would help a lot of people. She was only five, how could she know this?

Chapter Ten

All was well. Everything was still the same, or was it? We were back at the church in Portsmouth under the pulpit and Stokely had his ball. Biko hurriedly called his father on the phone to let him know where he was. When his father answered, he told Biko that they would be finished more quickly than they thought. They would meet him in the church sanctuary in ten minutes. By the time Biko and Stokely got back upstairs, they heard their parents leaving the meeting.

When Biko saw his father he ran up to him, grabbed him and gave him a big hug.

"I am sorry about my attitude. I will be better and help more."

His father laughed and said,

"You must really want to go swimming!"

At the same time, Stokely ran to their smiling mother and jumped into her arms. She almost lost her balance, but she just held him and smiled as she so often did. As we were all leaving together, the preacher asked everyone if we would like a tour of the hiding places on the Underground Railroad. Stokely spoke up and said,

"That's okay. We know where they are. Under the pulpit, behind the choir loft and in the attic. We have already seen them."

Before they could respond, I quickly added,

"Thank you very much. Maybe we can come back on another visit."

When the family got into the car, everyone started talking all at once. Stokely wanted gum.

I wanted to charge my phone and my parents wanted to discuss the will.

They said Ama would be very pleased. Miss Churchill left a scholarship for anyone who wanted to research the history of Emanuel and publish it. Ama was to be in charge of making the selection. She could choose anyone for the scholarship including family members. And then my mother unwrapped an item that was left for Ama. The paper was old and yellowed and the cord was thick, but frayed. When she finally got it undone, there was the old, iron cross that Stokely had dropped.

"Oh, this is amazing. What a treasure!"

My mother would never know just how amazing it was. Miss Churchill left a type written letter to Ama describing the gift:

Dear Brenda,

This has been in our family for many years. We highly value it. Since I have no children, I want you to have it. I think you will take care of it and understand the important message of freedom and determination that it carries. If you look closely, you will see an engraved message that got my family through many difficult times. *Trouble don't last always.* I hope you will remember it when times may become challenging in your own life. I love you and know that you and your family will continue in the tradition of sacrifice, wisdom and hope that our church teaches.

Love,

Miss Churchill

My mom let me see it. It was the same cross that was given to Stokely by Nathan. But how? Stokely had it when we were leaving and it fell onto the floor.

My mother cautioned Stokely,

"Be careful. That cross is old and very special. It was hand made from the builders of Emanuel with the left over iron from the staircase."

My father said,

"I think we should tell the story and share it with the National Museum of African American History and Culture in Washington. What do you think?"

Stokely said, *"It's mine."*

And then I said, "Stokely will probably let you share it, if we can finally go swimming."

"Right, Stokely?"

"Right, David!" he said with a giggle.

My father thought he was talking to him; I thought he was talking to me. And we both said,

"Well, trouble don't last always."

The adventure was over and I was glad to be with my wonderful family. I still don't know exactly how we got home. It surely had something to do with the special cross; it had something to do with faith and it had something to do with Stokely. I really did not need to know how we got home. I was just glad to know that we were at home and that our family would be safe and in the future, our people would be truly free.

Who ever thought I would become a freedom fighter? I guess I would soon learn if Stokely and I would have another special mission. Did you notice? Our names changed when we got back: Biko and Stokely. Somebody's mission was successful because we were both named after freedom fighters.

My mother said we were probably disappointed with the will because we were not going to be rich and I would still have to do my own chores. They stopped the car abruptly in the parking lot and both of my parents turned around in amazement, when I said,

"With the family I have, I am more than rich! And I want to do my own chores. There is dignity in work."

I guess I did learn a lot on my adventure and I was ready to help others on another mission whenever I was needed. It was good to know that no matter how bad things seem *"Trouble don't last always!"*

Maybe I could help others know that when they needed to know it most.

Epilogue

Before we could get going again, Ama was calling from Ghana. My Dad put her on the speaker and before we could say hello she asked me: *"Did you find any GOATs?"*

She laughed the way only Ama could and I wondered, what did Ama know about our vacation adventure?

She said there were seven Greatest of All Time heroes on our journey. I told her I knew them:

Nathan, Arthur, Bill, David, Stokely and me. She laughed some more. Our parents didn't know what we were talking about.

"You left one out!"

That's when Stokely yelled, *O!*

"Yes, Stokely. O was a reader. Her job was to read messages that were sent back and forth on the Underground Railroad. No one ever suspected her, because she was only five. O is short for Ora. Miss Ora Churchill!"

Fun Facts

This story is fiction, but there are many fun facts in it:

- Stokely and Biko really are brothers and they really do love each other. They live in Atlanta.

- They have a father named David, a grandfather named Bill and a grandmother they call Ama.

- Portsmouth is real and so is the church Emanuel AME. It was one of many stops on the Underground Railroad. It was Miss Churchill's church and she loved it.

- Mother Bethel AME Church in Philadelphia is real. It is on the oldest land continuously owned by African Americans in this country. And Biko really was in Erin's wedding there, when he was two.

- Miss Ora Churchill is real. She was a very strict teacher, who taught school for fifty years. She taught many of the children in Portsmouth, but she did not teach Ama. She did live across the street from Ama and was very fond of her.

- Miss Churchill's picture really is in the lobby of the Renaissance Hotel in Portsmouth.

- Segregation was legal in the South, but Miss Churchill lived long enough to see the laws change.

- Pocahontas was a Powhatan, which was a part of the Algonquian Indians in Virginia. The English colonizers took more and more of their land from them.

- Nathan and Arthur were not brothers, but their names were the names of great grandfathers. Both did live in different parts of North Carolina.

- CPR stands for cardiopulmonary resuscitation. It is an emergency procedure that can be useful in drowning and other situations where the heart has stopped.

- The Mason-Dixon Line is real. It separated Maryland, where enslavement was legal and Pennsylvania, where there was no enslavement.

- There were many abolitionists, who fought to end enslavement. Harriet Tubman and Frederick Douglass were two of them.

- The Emancipation Proclamation was signed by President Abraham Lincoln on January 1, 1863 and freed the enslaved, but there were exceptions. Interestingly, it did not free those enslaved in Portsmouth.

- Biko's great grandfather really was chastised by George Washington Carver and later he really did have professors from the Harlem Renaissance when he studied at Howard University.

- The National Museum of African American History and Culture is real. It is in Washington, D.C. Not only does it tell the stories of African Americans, but it has collected many family treasures from across the country.

- Ama really is wonderful! But then she wrote this book. She wrote this book for Biko. Remember, until the lion writes the story, the hunter will always be the hero. There are so many new *lionized* heroes in this story and there are many more heroes to discover!

Made in the USA
San Bernardino, CA
22 January 2020